# MYSTERY MINUTES

## VOLUME 2

## B. A. PAUL

# Contents

# FOREWORD

"What in the world?"

"Are you kidding me?"

"How did *that* happen?"

Not many days go by without one of these phrases—or a similar one—slipping from my mouth.

Because, as we all know, life is a mystery, full of twists, turns, and the utterly unexpected. My recent puzzles include the small, lumpy package left at the edge of the mattress from a favorite feline (it was, indeed, a dead mouse) or the bill that arrived a *few hundred dollars* over the expected baseline (rogue aging person with a new-to-her voice-controlled remote ordering repeated showings of Home Alone and Crocodile Dundee in HD—I kid you not).

We're always on the hunt for clues to solve what annoys us, but perhaps it's time for a break—away from why the clothes dryer sounds like a dying moose.

Away from why your son's yo-yos have been split in half and nailed to the shed floor.

Away from why the driveway security camera alerts you to

passing red dump trucks an entire street over but *not* the darkly shrouded stranger approaching the garage...

Okay, maybe that stranger thing needs addressing before you join the characters tucked inside the pages of Mystery Minutes Volume 2, but I digress.

Happy reading!

B. A. Paul

# LIFETIME VALUE

*First seen in Pulphouse Fiction Magazine, Issue 14, Lifetime Value explores the dark underworld of the filthy rich—and what they love to spend their dollars on the most.*

I'm good at what I do. That's why he chose me.

I close the green leather-bound ledger and lean back in the wooden office chair. One of those old-time designs. Heavy oak, swivel base, casters. Armrests permanently set at an unnatural height.

Mini rectangles of light illuminate the dark wood paneling along one wall, but the rays only make it two-thirds of the way down on a sunny day. Most days aren't sunny. I can see the occasional pair of feet walking by on the sidewalk above. Some heels clacking. Some tennis shoes pounding. Strolling or hurrying off to their destinations.

None the wiser of the goings-on here.

I reach for the metal lamp and twist the switch at the top of the shade. The heat from the bulb radiates through the scuffed black paint, burning my fingertips. I've been working a while.

Likewise for the black oscillating fan sitting on the massive desk opposite the lamp—the switch is hot, a complaint from spinning too long. Another relic. Metal blades. A near-frayed electrical cord that would send OSHA running for their clipboards and violation forms —if they knew. The kind of fan that would fetch pretty pennies at auction, money handed over by yuppies to decorate their apartments in things gone by.

Art deco, I think they call it. But that's not my area, décor.

I'm a book person. Numbers. Figures. I run my hand over the ledger and my heart sinks because I know what information lurks in those gold-gilded pages. I know every name. I've committed to memory every dollar sign and date. I'll need that information.

And I'll need it soon.

I stand and stretch, and my neck and lower back give satisfying pops. I really have been sitting here for quite some time. I glance at the wall opposite the desk at the round clock as I reach back for my ponytail and twist it into a tight bun on the top of my head. The clock has a white face, black numbers. Old school, hard-wired into the electric. Red second hand tumbling around and around in jerky rhythm.

When all is quiet and the fan blades are still, I can hear the clock's hum.

I walk across the room and make sure everything is just how he likes it.

The room is just so. He'll be pleased with the work I've accomplished.

If I didn't know any better, if I were watching myself on a screen from some other vantage point than the doorway of this undergrown den, I'd think this was a setting from one of those old detective movies. Antique and eclectic. Dusty and hazy. Right down to the office door with the frosted glass panel window inset. Fading white letters. OFFICE.

If I didn't know any better.

My dorm is on the fourth floor. I take the stairs up after locking the office. Steps worn with age, ever so slightly dented in the middles where the marble has given up after decades of foot traffic. I've taken to using the very sides of the steps. Where the angles are sharp, level. And where the marble still holds its original cut. I can move faster that way without fear of planting a foot awkwardly on one of those wavier steps.

So many trips up and down from the dorm. To the office. To the girls' hall.

I've cataloged all my movements and the locations of the waviest steps in my head as if they were an entry in the green ledger. Intimately familiar.

I round the landings on floors One and Two, which are quiet, then keep to the right as I scale another level. From the girls' hall on Three, giggles sneak under the closed metal fire doors. I pause for a moment on Three's landing. I'm not out of breath from the climb—I climb up and down these stairs all day. Every day. Doing his bidding.

Quite the contrary. My strength is at its peak.

No. I catch my breath because the giggles are misguided. Giggles over their new-found gifts. And they'll be happy playing dress up in new clothes and doing one another's nails in all shades of pinks and crimsons. Pulling blonde hair into sparkling barrettes and taming brunette curls with glittering headbands. Painting faces with the highest-quality makeup money can buy.

I know what gifts they've received. Every evening gown, right down to the maker and size for each of the sixteen girls. Every "spa day kit."

Because I bought those items. I hung the spa supplies, tucked into red satin drawstring bags, from each door's knob last night. I hung each evening gown from the ornate brass hooks he'd installed above and to the right of each door frame. So the gowns wouldn't wrinkle.

Because it's Auction Night. And the giggles will soon be stifled.

And I know this because this is my fourth Auction Night with him.

And I'm good at what I do.

And because this time, I know one of the sixteen from before. From before I was Melanie Hampshire.

I stand and listen as the laughter and surprised gasps die down, the girls retreating into their rooms to get ready for the big event. I reach out and touch the metal door, cold and stark gray, but I dare not enter their hall. Not yet.

I scale the remaining flight and open my set of metal doors on Four. My room is across from his. When he's here. And today, he's here. I see light spilling into the hallway and the shadows of movement as feet break the rays' path from under the door.

I turn to my dorm and open the door. It's never locked. I only need a key for the office.

And a set of keys for the rooms on Three.

I close the door behind me and lean on it. Not from fatigue or weariness—even though I've gotten little sleep over the last few nights. Preparing. Shopping. Keeping the books. I lean and breathe deeply because it's almost done.

When he'd chosen me, I thought I'd live on the third floor, but I didn't make that cut. After I saw the girls that did, I understood why. They are impeccable. Flawless. So perfect that in all actuality, the makeup I'd placed in some of their bags could have the opposite effect—toning down their beauty instead of accentuating it.

Me, not quite so much. I'm not bad looking. I was deemed worthy of the other position. Of his trusted—almost trusted—right-hand dorm room supervisor. He'd done his research. He'd found the information on me that I'd wanted him to find.

Melanie Hampshire. Near photographic memory. Quiet. Unattached with no family. Minimal social media footprint.

No one would miss Melanie. No one would miss me.

I went to the kitchenette and poured a glass of ice water and sat on the stool at the counter. The only stool, chrome legs and trim. Padded vinyl yellow seat in need of patching. I spin the glass on the counter and watch as condensation begins to form. I try to zone out, but it doesn't work.

I can't because I know what's happening under my feet one floor down.

At first, he had me placing signs all over the city. Professionally made advertisements for his modeling agency. A real, true-to-life agency. Complete with legal bookkeeping and portfolios and reviews from girls young and old. Boys young and old, too.

I take a sip and feel the cool water snake down to my stomach. I trace the sweaty tears on the glass. And then I turn from the tiny kitchenette to face the far wall of my dorm where my twin bed sits across from a mahogany armoire.

When I was a kid, I loved reading the Narnia books. Now, after 492 days of living in the dorm, I never want to see—or read about— any armoire ever again.

I approach the piece and swing open the door. It's taller than I am, and the space for the hanging clothes takes up half of the interior's width. The other half is filled with pull-out drawers with knobs in the shape of roses. Etched vines and leaves wiggle over the drawer fronts and on the doors and trim. I've traced them. Memorized them, as well.

He's left me a gift inside the armoire. One that he picked out. One that I'm to wear tonight while I keep his gold-gilded ledger down to the very last decimal point.

A simple black gown. Straight cut down to the hip area where it flares just a bit. A rim of dainty rhinestones trims the waist area. Elegant enough to stand by his side, but understated. As to not draw attention one way or the other from the main attractions.

From one of the rose knobs hangs a black satin choker with a single clear stone. In the closet, three more black gowns hang in silent tribute, all different cuts. One strapless. One spaghetti. One off-shoulder. Worn once each. I'd draped the chokers and necklaces for those evenings around the hangers and stored them with the gowns.

You'd think I would push the gowns as far back in the armoire as they could go. But I don't. They remind me that I'm here for a reason. That patience pays off. That diligence poured into every detail of this place, of him, of the girls, is not in vain.

The three black dresses remind me that I'm good at what I do.

Those three nights I count as losses. Three auctions. Fifty girls. Girls come and now gone. Girls dreaming of being molded into masterpieces at his hand. The Third Floor girls. How much better they were than the ones simply taking sessions on the Second Floor, simple headshots in the studios or three-pages portfolios for some other agency. The *Third Floor* girls are the ones that have his promise that *they* have promise. And potential.

And what a grand amount of money they will make over their lifetimes with their flawlessness. What a lavish lifestyle they'll enjoy. He promised.

And their lifetime value would just increase and increase...

I lay the gown on my bed and smooth the fabric. I retrieve the choker and open the single window above my futon. Outside my window there's a rusty fire escape that barely clings to the side of the building and drops into the alley below. But he knows I won't leave. I brush my hand over my left hip where the tracker sends him updates of my whereabouts.

I don't go anywhere where he doesn't know. Sometimes I sit with my right leg out of the window, dangling in freedom, while the left leg stays firmly inside the dorm room.

The girls under me don't need trackers. The allure of lavishness is enough to keep them chained.

He didn't know when he'd chosen me that I didn't need a tracker either. That I'd chosen him first. And I'm here to stay.

I reach outside the window where I'd loosened a nail from the wooden casing. I hang the choker there, on the rusty nail. And I dangle my right leg out and pray.

---

I shower, and while in the bathroom I can hear the rattle of the fire escape, but I dare not go toward the window. To see who came. To see a familiar face from my life before.

From before I was Melanie Hampshire.

My heart beats faster, and I will myself to calm. Thousands of trips up and down the marble staircase. Countless nights of sleepless planning. Hundreds of hours of prep.

All leading up to this night.

I dress in the gift he left. He has a way with sizes. The gown is a perfect fit. I return to the bathroom and blow dry my hair. Plain brown hair, somewhat frizzy. I trim a few frayed ends over the commode. I pull the locks up and into a tight bun and secure it with a rhinestone-tipped clip.

Makeup is next. To cover the freckles and fill in the tiny lines. More lines now than a year ago. Lines etched by extreme concentration on the ledger. On the building.

On him.

The freckles and the plainness. Why I'm not a Third Floor girl.

Satisfied with the image and brown eyes staring back at me, I leave the mirror and walk to the window, still open.

I reach out and feel for the choker. I remove it from its hanging spot and close the window. The breeze is a bit cooler now than it was an hour ago.

I go to the nightstand by my bed and turn on the switch. A lamp, black metal, similar but smaller than the one in the office. I hold the choker under the light. I see no flaws save a minuscule nick near a prong that holds the rhinestone—and now the microphone—in place.

Someone else on my team is good at what they do, too.

I unhook the clasp and wrap the piece around my neck and hook it in place. I go back to the mirror to examine the finished product. I can't see the nick when it's on my neck. I hope he won't be able to, either.

I slip into my black heels, glad that I'll be using the elevator this evening. Hoping I won't need the memorized map of stairs in the building. I step into the hallway and turn to face the dorm that's been my home for 492 days. The twin bed. Made with military corners. The futon. Rarely sat upon. Never unfolded. The kitchenette. Wiped and sanitized.

The window. My saving grace.

And I pull the door shut.

---

He meets me in the hallway and we walk to the elevator. He puts in his key and I step into the car with him. The silver doors slide shut. He examines my dress. My hair. He adjusts the rhinestone on my throat and I hold my breath for a millisecond. Then he smiles and nods.

I've passed the test.

We slip through the belly of the building down to the office. I wait in the elevator while he opens the office door and retrieves his ledger from the desk. Right where I'd left it. He joins me, slides his key into a different lock, and we ride up to the first floor. When *No. 1* lights up above our heads and the door slides open, we're in a new world.

The bustle of cocktail hour with tuxedoed waiters balancing silver trays of champagne and hors d' oeuvres is such a contrast to the Third Floor. And the photography studios on Second. It took my breath away the first time I saw it. And it takes my breath tonight.

He smiles and leads me through the fray of bodies and music and food to a room off the main ballroom. Rows of chairs covered in red velvet wait for their audience. A stack of bidding paddles waits on a table in the back. White. Round. With black numbers and smooth wooden handles.

He takes me and the ledger to the front podium. I open the book and turn to tonight's offerings.

Sixteen names.

Sixteen girls.

Sixteen "someone's daughters," all with their LV columns filled in.

And organized from lowest to highest lifetime value.

Whether used as models or call girls or sold some other way is none of his concern. Or mine—so I'm told. Every name in the ledger has a running total of monies spent for room, board, evening gowns, and photo shoots. But the LV column is most important for Auction Night. That's why the buyers come.

They want to bid on the girl with the highest possible lifetime value. He uses a top-secret set of calculations, developed by him, on every girl ever to come through the door. Those calculations determine whether a pretty face will be a Third Floor girl or simply get the standard package from the photography front of the Second Floor.

He used the calculation on me. He told me my LV was unimportant because I was good at what I did. He was to keep me. Indefinitely.

I take my seat in one of the three chairs on the stage as he retrieves the gavel and block set from the podium's cabinet. He positions them just so next to the ledger. I glance to my right. A doorway there leads to the elevator's hall. Where the girls will bypass the festivities in the ballroom and take a seat in one of the sixteen chairs that line the wall. Spotlights shine on these seats. Their rhinestones and glitter will sparkle and shine, hopefully catching the eye of someone with money.

Lots of money.

Four times I've been on this stage. Four auctions. Three down. One about to go. And the weight of the rhinestone's microphone presses the air out of my lungs.

---

The girls are seated in a line of sixteen. The one I know from before looks straight ahead. She's good at what she does, too.

Some would call us a team. Him and me. And the sixteen girls.

But the real team is her, me, and the unknown tech guru from my fire escape.

I'd chosen a choker similar to mine from the jewelry inventory for her. One with a stone and setting large enough for tech. I slipped it into her red satin drawstring kit, the one I'd placed outside her door last night in preparation for Auction Night. And I knew from before I was Melanie that there would be a nail, rusted or not I don't know, protruding from a Third Floor window casing. Just over the fire escape.

This girl. She lived directly under my feet.

I don't look at her now, except when I scan the entire row of young ladies, giving each of them the exact same count of attention so as not to draw attention. The glances understated as always. She crosses her left leg over her right and tucks them under her chair.

She's ready.

The third auction, the one that we'd missed on, the familiar face in the line of girls—a different face from this evening—had given the same signal, but something had gone wrong. And the auction went forward.

Major loss. I don't know what happened to the undercover girl. I only know her Lifetime Value number. It was high. She was sold.

He stands at the podium and adjusts the gooseneck on the microphone for his height. Tall. Muscular. Handsome. No aspiring model would say no to him. To his offers.

I'd asked him after the second auction why he insists on doing the auction himself. Why risk being seen when he usually stays in the background of the top two floors. And I'm the face in front of the ladies and the go-between.

He gave a charming grin and said Auction Night is his pet. His creation. And that demanded he be seen and remembered. To grow the business.

And that he trusted only me to keep careful care of the business and the girls in between the auctions because I was, well, forgettable.

And he'd put this in such a way that I almost took it as a compliment.

Almost.

I look to my right and scan the row of girls as the audience, bidders and their business cohorts, fill the red cushioned seats. Many have paddles. Some are drunk. Realization hits a few of the young women. But I bought them high-end makeup so the mascara doesn't smear when the tears start. Sparkling tears to match their glitter and stones.

The familiar face does well, blending in. Pretending to have just caught on to something that she's known for as long as I have. She wraps one arm around the midsection of her red evening gown. She brings her other hand up and rests it on her shoulder. I know she does this to move her fingers that much closer to the rhinestone choker. Others assume she's self-comforting in the realization of her fate. She blends in well. Even in glittering scarlet.

The seats are filled with eager bodies. He stands behind the podium, raises the hammer, then brings it down hard on the block.

The audience startles and hushes. The girl in the turquoise gown can't stifle her sob, but she's ignored by the horde. The girls on either side of her dare not move to comfort her.

He welcomes his guests. He ignores the merchandise. Treats them as such. As if they're inanimate objects. Which brings more sobbing. Because until today, he'd treated each one as if she were the only girl in the universe. Someone with value. Personal value to him.

He gives introductory rules, reminds them all of the contracts they'd signed before arriving, and begins the bidding.

My familiar lady in red glances in my direction and I catch this out of the corner of my eye. We allow the first girl in line to be sold. A relatively low LV, and she went quickly. Everyone's waiting for the higher values to come to the block.

The girls remain seated until the end when their owners will gather them and escort them out of the building. Never to be Third Floor girls again.

We allow the second girl's auction to proceed. A little more money changes hands. As he brings the gavel down and pronounces "sold," I see my teammate tap her choker.

*Please work this time.*

The third and fourth girls are sold.

He reads out loud the fifth's description. He highlights height, weight. Natural hair color. Eye color. Maintenance costs. And as he is about to disclose her LV figure to the audience, the back doors burst open.

And just like that, Auction Night is over.

---

I allow myself to be cuffed. As does she.

Others go with more of a tussle. Upstanding businessmen outed. Fathers found out. Someone's brother. Someone else's husband. A couple of wives. There are too many for metal cuffs. Some of them now wear standard black zip ties as they leave the building.

And he. He is to be free no more. A prisoner of his own making in a prison made by others. And certainly much less comfortable than the dorms of Third Floor.

In the squad car, the officer unlocks the cuffs. I gaze at the stars through the window. Sparkling like rhinestones. I reach up and let down my hair, relaxing a bit. I make sure they bring the ledger. I take off the choker. My hidden microphone captured enough of the auction to be proof. But the ledger was the real evidence.

And the testimonies of the fifteen young ladies we'd saved. Impeccable women. Flawless. Unforgettable.

And as I wait for the ride to the station, back to my life before I was Melanie Hampshire, I wonder where the other girls are. Likely no longer flawless or impeccable. I remember the three black dresses hanging in my armoire. Three auctions' worth of girls. Gone.

But I know all of their names. All the girls lost in the two information-gathering auctions. And the auction we blew. I know their vital statistics. Height, weight. Eye and hair color. I know their values. Their true values, not the digits and decimals in the LV column of the green ledger.

He'd told me I was forgettable.

But I haven't forgotten any of them.

I'm good at what I do.

# THE CIRCLE

*A whole new take on group therapy...*

The basement room fills slowly, as rooms like this usually do. I'm here first. I like to watch the people drag in after long days of work or family life or Netflix-and-raw-cookie-dough binges. I compare my journey to the stages of everyone else. Better than the man who always wears concert t-shirts. Much worse off than the CEO, ex-military gal likely already immune to certain stressors given the nature of her work—so I don't beat myself up too badly. She has a leg up on me, after all.

Mostly, I think I've hit a happy middle. At least with this circle of folks. Not much worse off than many. Not much better than the rest. Right in the middle.

I'd been much better off than all the other participants in the last circle of chairs I sat in—even the seats were better. Padded cushions.

I had left that group fairly quickly. Hard to be pulled up to a higher level of thinking when you're already five steps ahead of the whole pack. My process required more depth. More lines of thought that I'd not explored. The only way to grow.

The plastic chairs' metal legs moan across the cement floor as one by one the participants scoot and arrange and vie for a favored spot in the circle. Mostly women at these things. Swollen eyes and lifeless complexions. Longer hair pulled back in lazy ponytails. A few men, though, likely a little grayer around the temples and in the facial hair than they were this time last year.

I know I am. With any more pigment loss, I'll be snow-white in eight months.

A little grayer around the temples. A little saggier under the eyelids. It's the hazard pay that we dish out to the great tragedies in our life.

Funny how tragedy can seep into skin cells, into hair follicles. Changing the very fabric of one's appearance. Organs pay a price, too. People in these circles speak of antacid meds and similar concoctions like during the breaks and before and after the sessions start. Sometimes, the conversations are nothing more than consumer alerts:

Try this one. No, that one doesn't work. I'm a big fan of... Fill in the blank with the latest and greatest acid blockers and over-the-counter sleep aids.

And then there's the harder-core stuff. What we all warn each other not to do, but most have tried some variation nonetheless. Unchecked alcohol consumption. Street drugs. Too many prescriptions from doctor hopping.

Hushed whispers toss between a few participants before our fearless, albeit damaged, leader arrives to organize us into one cohesive gripe fest. Whispers only, as though the basement of the recreation club is hallowed ground. Whispers as though fully audible speech would send another member into the throes of anguish.

Like we all aren't already there.

Heavy footsteps on the wooden stairs. My last group had two people in wheelchairs, so the Methodist church across town made their accessible-friendly sanctuary available twice a week. That was nice of them. But they didn't allow food or drink in their newly renovated space. So, those that wished to cleanse sorrow via coffee and pies had something else to grieve.

That was the same group that had proved me to be more advanced than I'd imagined. Comparatively speaking. So I'd left that one after only a few weeks. I do think about those folks sometimes. Baring their souls in those padded seats with not even a powdered doughnut to look forward to afterward.

I like this anonymous group. Not because of the sweets and treats, but because of that happy medium. I like blending. While tragedy paints hair gray and sags the skin, it often hangs a neon sign on your forehead that says "I'm in pain. Ask me about it." And after being out in the universe and having people ask so much, it's nice to be in the middle.

Unseen.

Unasked.

Only participate if you want to.

The footsteps belong to Seth. He brought the sweets. I'd started the coffee pot as soon as I got here. Pamela had asked the first ones in if they'd handle that task. I didn't mind. Gave me something to do while I waited and watched the people. I don't drink the stuff. Makes me jittery. I have trouble sleeping anyway. Too wired.

The ancient pot starts popping and sizzling, sending wafts of smoky brew into the room. Seth lays out the mini cheesecake bites on the refreshment table. I have my eye on the white chocolate bit with the tiny raspberry icing curl. I'd bought a tray like it last week. To do my Netflix-and-binge-cheesecake-bites marathon. I know how that tiny raspberry curl melts on the tongue, lighting up tangy and sweet taste buds simultaneously.

I nod my approval to Seth. He nods back. Aside from our dessert choices and the losses we've suffered, Seth and I would never run in the same circles. Only this slowly forming circle of chairs in this random basement.

Pamela comes down the steps. I know it's her because she always wears boots with heels that clack-scoot across the wooden steps then click on the concrete. This is my sixth time here. Fourth time being the first to arrive. I'm learning footsteps. Attention to detail seems to be heightened after everything I've been through.

The members who had been reverent with their whispers elevate their voices over the extra bodies and scooting chairs and heels on concrete. Pamela shakes a few hands and motions for us to get started.

Two minutes past our scheduled start time. I don't know if anyone but me notices that detail.

"Good evening. Let's open in a moment of silence." Pamela would prefer to outright pray, I think, but the mix of beliefs—or lack thereof—represented here forces her to take this route. As the group falls in line, the clock behind me pounds out the seconds. Time echoes off the bare cinderblock walls. The coffee pot gives another pop and bubble. I try to focus on that. The smell. The steam.

Most people bow their heads and close their eyes. Some bow, but don't close. They look down at their crotches or the floor.

I do neither.

Head up. Eyes wide open. Always watching. Waiting for the next detail, sound, or alarm.

Pamela suggested I get checked out for PTSD. Maybe I will. Someday.

I scan the group, careful to note anyone like me disrespectful enough to gawk around. Eye contact in this context would be like speaking in an elevator that's only traveling two floors. It's a face-forward, mouth-shut kind of moment. No one else is looking, though, so I shift silently in my orange plastic seat and let my eyes linger over the group.

Ten strong tonight. There were twelve last week.

I wonder what they think about with bowed heads and closed eyes. Are they communing with their higher power? Maybe they think about the ones they've lost. Maybe their minds are simply empty, all mental capacity spent on surviving another week. Another day. Another half hour.

Tragedy does that too. It cuts time into odd chunks to be overcome. The fresher and more severe the loss, the smaller the chunks. Minute by minute. Minutes to hours. Hours to afternoons or evenings. And so on.

Until day to day. Then week to week.

Until the ticking of the clock and the squares on the calendar with their sharp right angles fall into a new proper place as background noise. Or a simple harmless sheet of paper marking away time while it dangles from the Santa Maria Island tourist magnet on the front of the refrigerator...

And there. That detail. Those blasted magnets from her trips. And her last trip... She loves those magnets. And the photos that come from frolicking in the waves with Dad and the joy she gets from retelling their adventures.

One last trip.

I hate grief. But coming here. With these people. I understand it better. I appreciate it more than those who skip this step and go it alone without thought about what will happen once something happens.

Once they make something happen. Or simply let it happen.

Whichever the case.

Pam raises her head and greets us once more. As if that silent moment erased her first greeting. There are no new faces tonight. No new depressed griever to introduce to the rest of the depressed grievers. So she gets right to it.

"Who'd like to start this evening? Share any new triumphs? New fears?"

A few people shift their feet, uncross one leg and then re-crossing the opposite leg. Some people look over the heads of those in front of them to the bare wall. I have a view of the stairs. I prefer to watch the exits and try to never sit with my back facing one. Exposed. Vulnerable.

One brave soul opens into a mundane retelling of the last few days. Work. Meals. Sleep. Then gets to the point of how cruel life is that it marches right on. Unyielding with the dirty dishes and laundry piles. Why couldn't it have more respect? Pause. Have the sun stand still while we all—I like how she included the entire group in her soliloquy—while *we all* take a breath and deal. This one, Becky, lost her husband to a drunk driver. Now she's the widowed mother of two boys who desperately need discipline from a father figure.

"Thank you, Becky. It is unfair. It makes us feel so tiny, doesn't it? That things continue on when we're hurting so badly?" Pamela digs in her ever-handy giant canvas bag for the square, pink box of tissues —lotion free—and hands it to Phillip who starts the box around the circle like a hot potato.

How interesting. Some people pass the box quickly. Resolved to keep the tears bottled up. Some people take three or four, even though the saline streams haven't started flowing.

Yet.

Becky takes three and cleans herself up. The box reaches me. I hesitate for a microsecond. I haven't cried in ages. Don't know when I'll cry again, but it won't be tonight. I'll stay in the middle. Somber, quiet. No tears. I think it's the best way to blend in.

And I like the middle.

I pass the box back to Pamela and she tucks it under her chair. "Ray, would you like to say something tonight? It's been a few weeks." She pats my knee. The tap ripples down to my toes and up into my throat. To stay in the middle, I know I have to contribute. Carefully contribute. And without too much—or too little—protest.

So I stall, if only for ten echoey seconds. I feel the others' eyes on me. Waiting. Wondering. Patient. They've all been in my shoes. A few haven't heard me speak yet. They only know my name. And that my "it" is my mom.

It.

That tiny little pronoun that means so much in contexts like this one.

*It.*

There's the chunk of time and life and memories before *it.*

There's the chunk of time and life and memories after *it.*

It becomes the most important event in the universe. For a while. Until the dulling happens and the it becomes more of a flat sepia photograph and less of a three-dimensional technicolor virtual reality.

I take a breath. "Well. I guess I'm struggling mostly with guilt this week."

"Guilt?"

*Careful, Ray.* "Yeah. I'm this middle-aged man who misses his mother. Lots of guys my age have dead parents. But they weren't... didn't"

"Most people don't lose their loved one so tragically."

I nod. She nods, prodding me to continue. Deepen the connection by baring more of my soul. I look down at my shoes and continue. "Mom calls me all the time. Bugs me to death. At any given moment my phone has twelve missed calls and they're all from her.

Dad sometimes calls, but it's always Mom who..." I pause for effect. And to figure out a direction. I should've had this one planned out better.

I glance up at eager faces. Eager for that connection. That similarity. They must wonder what this man means by guilt? Does he carry the same guilt? Should *I* feel guilty?

And some of them do feel guilt. If Dan had come home from work five minutes earlier, maybe his little girl would've skipped the playtime in the backyard to give her daddy a hug and never stepped on the hornets' nest. Dan feels guilty.

Maybe if Lorrianne had chosen couples' counseling over therapy with a bartender her husband wouldn't have resurrected his smoking habit to dull his misery. And maybe the cancer wouldn't have suffocated him. Lorrianne feels guilty.

Those ever-haunting I-should'ves. I-could'ves.

I feel guilt. That's why I'm here. To work it out. To hear how others work it out. To watch the path that grief puts one on and know what may lie ahead for me.

Everyone in this circle struggles with past guilt. And present guilt. I'm working on future guilt, but they can't know that. I have to stay in the middle...

"Mom and Dad go to Santa Maria Island every other summer. This will be the summer. And she always buys another fridge magnet to add to her collection," I say. "That will be her last magnet." I get to the point. "I wish my Mom would die of cancer. Or old age. Or anything else but..."

"But how she did die."

I nod at Pamela's observation.

"And what kind of a son am I that I would wish my parent to die of cancer?" I glance at Lorrianne who's now using one of her two tissues to dab at her eyes. She doesn't look at me. I can't blame her.

"Does anyone have any thoughts? Anyone ever felt something similar?"

Suzanne mentions how she could've accepted a terminal physical diagnosis and untimely passing of her teenage son rather than the fact that he committed suicide. She gets where I'm coming from. I nod at her. She gives one of those microsecond half smiles.

If they get where I'm coming from, I can stay hidden in the middle.

The group goes quiet. Most look to Pamela to get us going again.

"This may be a little off the present topic, Ray, but I do have an observation."

That jarring, like the jarring from her pat on my knee, starts again deep in my gut. What will she bring to the surface? Will I need the pink tissue box or the exit? I realize my chest hurts because I'm holding my breath. I exhale.

She continues. "Did you catch that you're still using present tense?"

I stare at her. I'm frozen. No. No I did not. Catch that.

She must see my scared eyes and pats my knee. "It's quite alright and it's quite common. I've just not seen someone use present-tense verbs quite this long."

Seth spoke up. "It took me weeks to stop that. I think I stopped a month after the funeral." He'll surely save me the white chocolate cheesecake bite now. At least slip me the raspberry curl on top.

Becky now. "Mine too. Like Seth's. The closure of the ceremony put the whole thing in the past. No less pain, but maybe acceptance?" She was reaching. Trying to sound therapeutic and failing miserably. But the group is nothing if not forgiving.

"Mine was quick. I saw how the cancer ate him little by little. So I knew it was coming. Maybe that's why." Lorrianne referring to her chain-smoking husband. Forgiving me of bringing up cancer.

I breathe deeply, allowing the oxygen to clear my head. Stay the course. In the middle. Seen but unseen.

"We won't—didn't have a service." I see understanding flood their faces. That must be the reason, they think. A collective thought. Group mentality. A unified understanding.

But they understand nothing.

Present tense. What an oversight. No one had ever brought this up with me before. And I've been in lots of circles with lots of people sharper than Pamela and Seth.

I try to shake off my mistake. "Her body... Dad won't—can't handle the thought of the ligature marks. Too much makeup will—would have been needed." I struggle with the wording. I can't believe no one caught this. I'm almost ready for the pink box. Or to bolt toward the stairway.

I aim my eyes up and to the right onto the bare wall. Past it, actually. Up into the gymnasium above us. Out into the street beyond. Out east to Mom's house. Where she cooks dinner tonight and dotes over Dad and rearranges those blasted fridge magnets. And no doubt she's called me ten times since tonight's circle started. I'll have to clear my cache and memory card.

Again.

I'm still not ready. Clearly more time is needed.

"Anyway, they haven't caught the guy."

"Yet," Pamela says. "They haven't caught the guy yet."

Lots of nods.

"And I noticed you're trying to change your wording now. Be patient with yourself. These things take time. Lean on us. We'll help you through."

"Thanks." I nod toward the tissue box, force my dry eyes to drip a little, and Pamela hands me the tissues while she urges a fellow griever to share.

The circle moves like hands of a clock. And in an hour, the sharing is over. I get pats on the shoulder. I give pats on other shoulders.

"Here, Ray." Seth hands me the white chocolate cheesecake bite on a white paper napkin. I decline the cup of coffee. I thank him.

Still holding the treat, I thank Pamela for her time. I ease my way to the corner of the room and watch near the base of the steps as the others mingle and continue sharing and patting and wiping tears. I won't be back here again.

I may have lost my hiding place in the middle. But, I think after several of these groups, I've learned what happens on the other end of loss. For those victims of death and all its ugliness. For those victims that must endure and overcome the chunks of time. Until the dulling happens.

I picture Dad coming to one of these after it happens. Not this particular group, of course. I'll find one for him a couple of towns over. Find a way to convince him better groups are worth the drive.

When he's ready. I won't push.

I turn my back to my fellow circle members and scale the steps. Into the sweat and old leather of the recreation hall's small gym. Out into the warm, starry night. I'm careful not to squash the cheesecake as I slide into the driver's seat of my SUV.

I lay the dessert in my lap.

I adjust the rearview mirror. I've lowered the backrow seats into the floor.

I've lined the back with heavy plastic. The bag next to me contains all I need to make an end of her. Painless. Quick.

Unlike the guilt I'll feel. But I know how to deal with it now. I've had the therapy beforehand.

I did these things—lowered the seats, lined the plastic, filled the bag—this morning in the privacy of my garage. I guess I always knew tonight would be my last night in the circle.

If I had any doubts, Pamela took them from me with the verb thing.

I pick off the raspberry curl from the top of the treat. I let it melt on my tongue. My senses have been heightened for days. Weeks. And how amazing that something so simple and small can light up taste buds and pleasure centers, melting away doubts and fear.

I swallow the sweet nectar and start the engine. Aim the SUV east toward my parents' home.

If I still need a circle when Dad's time approaches, I'll be sure to use the past tense in my narratives.

In my new circle. With faces I've not seen before, but grief I'll know well.

I'll stay in the middle of the pack.

I'll arrive first and brew the coffee.

And I'll be sure to bring the little cheesecake bites with the raspberry-flavored curls.

# THE SONG OF IVORY

*Young Tara grew up in the prison of her mother's mental illness, the bars of her cell reinforced with delusions and secrets too thick to bend. Will the understanding of the depths of her mother's dysfunction motivate her to break free before it's too late—or is Tara destined to fulfill the role cast for her in this twisted parody?*

My mother believes herself to be Scarlett O'Hara. And Father plays along.

I slip the white chiffon's spaghetti straps off the plush satin hanger and hold at arm's length this dress chosen to contrast against my tanned skin and dark hair—and against the ebony black piano. In a few moments, Miriam will help me tie a red satin ribbon in an ostentatious bow around my waist. Another ribbon, thinner and dotted with dainty white pearls braided into my locks, will complete the ensemble.

I'm surprised Mother doesn't make me wear a corset.

I smooth the dress flat on my four-poster bed and lie back to stare at the canopy one last time. Everything about our home is ostentatious. Draperies. Ruffles. Antebellum South artifacts fit more for a museum than a home. Heavy furniture in velvets and velours. Some original. Some replicas.

All Gone-With-The-Freakin'-Wind style. Right down to my name.

Tara.

I'm anything but antebellum. And we don't live in the south. Not one hint of a southern drawl. I can't even fake a drawl.

I prefer cell phones and superhero movies in high definition. We have one television in the sitting room tucked behind the heavy oak doors of an antique armoire. If you didn't know it was there, you'd never know it was there. And it's only wired to a DVD player. No cable or Netflix services for Tara. We only have one movie in the house—well, several copies of the same movie. All other contraband must be snuck onto our property and properly stowed away behind winter coats and loose floorboards until Mother falls into her fragile state of fitful sleep and Father retires to the liquor cabinet.

Half the time when my parents say my name, I'm not sure if they're speaking to me, about me, or about our three-acre property (which Mother also named Tara) in the upper peninsula of Michigan.

We have a large house, yes, and some would declare such a massive abode an "estate." But that's not what Mother sees when she looks out her window. She sees a plantation like on the movie set. Sprawling hills, fields full of dark farmhands, sunsets painted with technicolor clouds. Every detail matching and morphing between scenery described in the novel and the Tara of the silver screen.

Right down to the family graveyard.

And the rest of us *must* see it, too. Or we pay dearly.

I cross my arms over my stomach and will the churning to stop. I don't get nervous before these mid-morning recitals. Twice a year, year after year, Mother parades her uppity group of hens onto our "estate" and marches me to the piano. Put on display.

After the second year of this, I stopped caring what the chattering ladies thought of my occasional missed note on some pre-Civil war era piece. So the nerves had stopped firing acid into my stomach.

But today, I have acid by the gallons. I swing my head and shoulders over the side of the mattress and pull up the dust ruffle to peer under the bed. Half-hanging upside down, the blood rushes to my temples. I reach underneath and feel the canvas strap of my backpack, packed last night with a few staples from the kitchen and my dresser drawers. I swing back up longways next to the ball gown and let the blood settle to its rightful position as I lie with my eyes closed and inhale deeply, then exhale as slowly as I can.

I stand and stretch. I check that my travel clothes still hang in the closet within easy reach, even though I've checked five times already. My post-recital clothes, for when I take off the last ball gown I'll ever wear. Dark blue denim jeans, long-sleeved gray T-shirt with the Ghostbusters emblem plastered across the chest, tan hiking boots. A heavy brown jacket, relieved from its post from the back of Father's closet, now stands sentinel over the other pieces in my closet. I dry my sweaty hands with the jacket's sleeve.

I let the musical score run through my head as an imaginary metronome sways out the timing of the notes. Every second important. Every second matters to the rhythm of the score. I stand in the middle of my bedroom and stretch out my arms to glide over imaginary keys, my fingers running through the piece. Muscle memory now. An easy piece, really, with the years of lessons—since the time my feet wouldn't reach the pedals and swung freely under the bench. Since before my fingers were long enough to grace the keys in proper form. How oblivious that small child had been. Wanting to make Mother proud. Yearning for Father's arms and tight embrace and to hear him call my nickname with such pride. *Ivory.*

I think of the thousands of hours of practice until the truth became clear. That all wasn't right with Mother. That all the training had simply been to appease her dangerous delusion.

I shake off the intrusive past and turn again to the chiffon resting patiently on the bed. I hear Miriam's footsteps outside my room. I close the closet door after I dry my hands again on Father's jacket. Today I'm nervous, and rightfully so.

This is my last recital. The last time my fingers will pound out Tara's Theme.

The last time I'll hear Father utter my nickname.

*Ivory.*

Because I refuse to be Scarlett O'Hara's prisoner.

Even if she is my mother.

---

As Miriam tugs and tucks the waist ribbon just so around my midsection and wrestles the bow into perfect loops, I gaze out the window at the newly budded maple trees spanning the yard and try to remember that moment when I realized my family was epically screwed. That I had been born into a circus instead of a loving unit. A similar feeling to when I realized there was no Santa Claus; I was in early grade school, but I can't pinpoint exactly when. My classmate Alicia had told me, but I wasn't really upset because, somehow, I'd already known.

Same with Mother's delusions. And then with Father's. I knew down deep.

Miriam starts on my hair. Pulling and tugging until my scalp hurts. Mother wanted me to call this lady "Mammy." But Miriam rolled her eyes and refused. Miriam is as white as any United States president, all but the one, anyway, and she is not our slave. Come to find out later, she'd been planted in our home by my concerned aunt when Mother found out she was pregnant with me. Miriam is a mental health nurse. Sent more to watch over little Tara than to cure my mother, but she fit the part of household servant well.

And it kept Mother calm. To have a Mammy just like Scarlett.

I realized Mother was ill during our weekly viewing of *Gone with the Wind*. We were watching that scene where Scarlett drives the buggy through Shantytown and a man attacks her. Mother flinched and cried right along with the lady on the screen, curling herself up into a ball. Father swept into the sitting room when Mother's cries had escalated to screams and scooped her into his arms and carried her off to her bedroom—a separate bedroom from his—and called Miriam for help.

I'd been left on the davenport. Shaken and alone. Alicia told me the next day no one calls couches davenports. And no one watches *Gone with the Wind* every week. Let alone had *that* tale as a childhood bedtime story. And no one our age refers to their parents as Mother and Father.

Something was wrong.

That was in middle school. About six years ago.

I thank Miriam. She gives me a quick squeeze on the shoulders and tells me I'll be great today. I thank her a second time, but this time I square up and look her straight in the eyes. "Really. Thank you for everything you've done for me. And my family."

She gives me an odd look, nods and then leaves the room.

This thank you serves as my goodbye to the woman who cared for me more than my own mother. Even if she did it for a paycheck.

I examine my image in the oval standing mirror. Picture-perfect.

White dress. Red ribbons. I don't wear rouge. Mother will pinch my cheeks before I'm presented to the crowd to blush them up.

And I'll let her. Because that interaction will serve as my last goodbye to Miss Scarlett.

As I wait for my cue to descend our staircase and greet the guests downstairs, a soft knock at my door signals the arrival of my father. I open it. He kisses my cheek and we sit on the end of the canopy bed.

"You look lovely, my bonnie lass. Just lovely."

I thank him and take his hand. I twist his worn golden wedding band around on his finger. He looks older today. He'd started looking much older than his years about ten years ago. Mother's illness had worn him down.

And then he'd joined her.

I'd once asked him why mother hadn't named me Bonnie. I had the dark hair like the child in the movie. It had made no sense to me that Tara won out when she'd already named our home that. A home my father had spent a slice of his inheritance on to acquire for her.

"You were supposed to be a boy. She was hoping for a daughter later on."

That reply likewise made no sense to me at the time, but I didn't press. I started to understand her illness when I entered middle school—or at least I had an awareness of it thanks to Alicia. A couple of years after, I learned you can't apply logic to an illogical mind. I leaned on Miriam more so in my teen years, and I was grateful my aunt paid for her services. Miriam had spoken with me many times about my parents. She'd used some fancy psychology terminology, but basically, they'd created an imaginary world for themselves—and for me—and if we didn't play along, things could go downhill fast.

But Miriam had no clue how far downhill things had gone before she ever came to work at Tara. And my aunt didn't know, either.

I'd only learned of the real horrors just six months ago.

Mr. Avery knew. He'd assigned our class an English paper. One that should've been completed with canned responses to inflate grades and egos and impress the teacher. It was that time machine bit. "If you could go back and change anything in the past, what would it be?" I took a chance and told him the truth.

My time machine would sling me to Margaret Mitchell's time. To destroy the manuscript or otherwise sabotage her progress. Because if the novel were never written, maybe my parents and I would have a normal existence.

Mr. Avery pulled me aside after he'd graded the paper. He'd given me an A.

And he'd given me a way out.

I lean my head on my father's shoulder and will my tears to stay behind my eyelids. We just sit here on the bed in the quiet. He needs that from me, I think. A quiet presence. Mother is anything but.

I'm grateful for family money. A series of wise investments in automobiles and aircrafts a generation or two ago had left my father and aunt very comfortable. Or I'd be on the street because both of my parents would be in jail.

What a butterfly effect. Because my grandfather had economic smarts and endowed his children with a small fortune, my mother, Miss Scarlett to the bone, had been attracted to my father for the financial gain it afforded her.

I wonder if Grandfather would've changed his will if he'd have known what would become of his grandsons.

Or to me.

Father stands and rubs the back of his neck. He walks to my dresser and runs his hands over my award certificates and diploma. I graduated high school last week. For this, I will be eternally grateful for Miriam's intervention. Mother had wanted to hire a tutor and keep me sequestered at Tara. Miriam said I'd be better served in the "system." School was my only respite from the madness at home, and I took full advantage of it. Graduated with honors.

And at school, I'd found my savior.

I've always known I'd leave Tara someday. And six months ago, that day all the twisted puzzle pieces aligned, I knew I would never come back.

A quiver runs through the deepest part of me, beyond my stomach, closer to my spine, as I watch Father examine my awards. And as I think about Mr. Avery.

"You did well, Ivory."

"Thank you, Father." I stand and pick up my high heels. It's almost time. I meet him at the dresser and push up on tiptoes to give him a peck on the cheek.

And this serves as my final goodbye to this fractured man.

After Father leaves the room, I place my heels just outside the door in the hallway. I return to the bed and pull the backpack from its hiding place and replace the ruffle. I drape the pack over my shoulder carefully so as not to mar the dainty straps of my dress. I retrieve my post-recital clothes from the closet and toss them over my arm, pick up the boots, and softly close the closet door. I look over the room before stepping into the hallway. This is my third goodbye— Miriam, Father, this room—in less than an hour.

Three down. Three to go.

I tiptoe to the back staircase and descend barefoot with my load to the back entryway. A breeze greets me through the open window. It smells of locust blossoms and freedom. I'm glad the spring rains have held off.

Two shovels lean against the corner, spilling tiny remnants of their work onto the wooden floor. Mother and Father have plans for me after the recital. Miriam is clueless or the police would be here.

But I can't call anyone. And logic doesn't apply in this situation. No one would understand. And they are my parents. And I think I love them. Or at least the idea of them.

Even if they wanted a third boy.

I remove the lid to the large basket. Three months ago, I'd accompanied Father to a flea market. We spotted this old woven basket that stood as tall as my hips and as wide as a piano bench. I'd never asked for anything on these trips. We were hunting treasure for Mother, and none of it appealed to me. But I wanted the basket. I needed it.

He didn't think Mother would approve. But I hung on his arm and blinked at him the way I'd seen her do so many times to get her way. He caved.

I'd felt a rush of power I'd not experienced before. Doing something for myself. Outside of the will of Scarlett.

Mother didn't like it, but I told her it would hide my ugly tennis shoes so I didn't have to bring them all the way into the house. And she caved. I peer into the empty basket and drop in my backpack first, then layer in the jacket, boots, shirt and pants. Every second will matter, so the order is important. I replace the lid and give the shovels the finger before I turn to the staircase.

I scamper up the steps and slide into my heels waiting patiently for me at my closed door. As I tuck an unruly strand of hair back into the braid, Miriam comes up the main staircase and smiles. "It's time, my dear."

I smile at her. My heart pounds. If she'd been a few seconds earlier, I'd have been caught.

Every second counts.

I follow Miriam with delicate, poised steps and perfect posture down the staircase and onto the landing. The great room bustles with guests. More this time than before. But that's not my worry.

Mother comes from her thriving milieu, arms outstretched. She's dressed in an Irish green dress, floor length, all lace and ruffles and poof. She wears a comb boasting pearls and tufts of white and green feathers in her auburn and gray hair. The other ladies passing in the background are dressed similarly. The men are in old fashioned multi-piece suits. Walking canes and parasols abound.

The guests think this a costume party of sorts.

To Mother, it's real life.

To me, it's purgatory.

She places her pale, icy hands on my bare shoulders and holds me at arm's length. "Tara. It's time." She kisses me on the forehead.

With both hands she reaches up and pinches my cheeks hard and then rubs along the cheekbone.

I give her a peck on each cheek.

Four farewells down. Two to go.

I turn to face the room. Vaulted ceilings, heavy goldenrod draperies, and patterned wallpaper give the place a funeral home feel. I guess that's fitting. Faces I've seen before smile and nod in approval. Some faces are new.

One face, slightly masked under the wide-brimmed dress hat, belongs to my savior.

Mr. Avery is blending in well.

I turn to the baby grand. Mother has placed an ostentatious display of daffodils, white roses, and ferns on the piano's lid. I slide down to the bench. Adjust my dress. Position my feet. Make that last micro-correction to my posture and place my hands on the keys.

I close my eyes and picture my metronome, but not the one with the oak casing and simple metal pendulum used during my practices for over a decade.

I reset the one I created over the last few months, piece by breath-taking piece. The casing is made of shimmering ebony—so black it's almost purple in some of my mind's rays. The pendulum is carved from the finest ivory with intricate lacy filigrees. The sliding weight is a solid ruby.

I reset this metronome in my head to sway out the beats until the recital is over. Until all the notes pour out of my fingers and onto the black and white rectangles for the last time. Until every breathing being on Tara's grounds stands in ovation and I take my next-to-final bow.

When Father calls me *Ivory* one last time.

I rush out the back of the kitchen, leaving the pile of brown-paper-wrapped long-stem roses—minus two red ones—on the counter. The flowers served as my excuse for stepping away from the recital. The roses needed water. Miriam offered, but I told her I needed some air. She understood.

And I need to leave now, even if I have to bypass air and hold my breath for the next several counts. Taking the roses cost me a few seconds. But these are my last two goodbyes. The ones that really matter.

I leave my heels in the kitchen and pad quickly around to the back entryway. I toss the lid off the basket and pull on my jeans underneath the white chiffon. A quick glance over my shoulder to be sure I'm alone—because every second counts and the ruby weight and ivory pendulum swing so fast, pink rays burst from the motion. I pull off the dress and pull on Ghostbusters. Boots are next, I don't have time to tie them. Jacket on. Backpack slung. Roses in hand. Then past the shovels and out the door.

I sprint toward the tree line, toward the boundary of our property.

Toward the gravesite.

A few hundred yards and I'm not winded. Mr. Avery suggested I take PE again my final semester. Even though I didn't need that credit. Mr. Avery was right.

My savior. He's left the truck he'd taught me to drive waiting for me past the tree line on a lonely country road. Keys under the seat. A wad of cash in the glovebox. A map to freedom. I can hear the engine grind to life as I turn the keys. It nearly drowns out the ticking of the ivory metronome, but I need a few more seconds before I bolt.

I kneel beneath the oak tree, the noon sun sprinkling welcoming warm yellows through the rustling leaves. This tree, this spot, can't be seen from the front of the home where the festivities continue.

Four fading headstones, simple concrete rounded rectangles, were here when father bought the place. Resting places belonging to owners long since forgotten. But they served as surrogates, I believe, for the gravesites of Tara's families.

The other three headstones are newer. Sharp white rectangles not yet worn with the wind and weather. Like three piano keys torn from the keyboard and wedged into the earth, the space between them serving as the blacks.

Two markers have the beginning and ending dates—dates spaced much too closely together.

I turn to the third headstone. It's a blank canvas. Patiently guarding the freshly dug pit. A shallow grave.

The events of the last six months, the realizations, the nightmares, the training and preparation. All of it, comes rushing back. I look over my shoulder. No one's coming. No one's missed me yet. My metronome grows impatient. Ivory and ruby in hypnotic sway.

The real Scarlett had three brothers. All died newborns.

*My* Scarlett had no brothers. But she did have two sons. That's when her morphing and matching of novel and film took an ugly turn. And it took my father with it. Covering Mother's sins. Helping her, even. There were *two* shovels.

Miriam doesn't know. Aunt doesn't know.

But I know. I think I always have.

I let the tears escape as I look into the pit. The pit meant for Scarlett's third brother. Mother's third boy. I was supposed to be that boy. I *am* that boy in her mind.

And in Father's.

And their gravesite nestled on the Tara Plantation isn't complete.

I run my finger over the names and lay the blooms on my baby brothers' graves. Final goodbyes to two brothers I never met.

I unzip my pack and pull out my practice metronome. I stand and glance over my shoulder at home one last time.

I hurl the oaken timer into the pit, and as it shatters against the hard, brown clods so does the ebony and ivory metronome in my head, the ruby splintering into a dozen sharp red shards. The cords holding me here begin to break and fall away. I feel lighter. I take to the tree line.

Ivory's song is about to begin.

# The Compliment Box

*Newly widowed Willa organizes and attends what may well be her final school reunion in her tiny hometown. However, a chance encounter with her old rival along with her plus one will rock Willa's world to its core...*

Willa Everly propped the chalkboard nameplate against the last box and stepped back to assess her progress. She and the rest of the decorating committee, all three of them, had transformed the Nulltown Nighthawks' gymnasium into a festive fifties-style throwback for the class reunion. It hadn't been an easy task. And the nag of the bunch, Edith Jones, had complained bitterly through the whole activity. "Why must we decorate for the fifties when we graduated late sixties? It doesn't make logical sense."

But they had to put up with her because out of their graduating class of eighteen students, only twelve were left to carry on and remember. With their spouses, the ones of those that were still living, and the three teachers that RSVP'd, the total head count for the reunion was twenty-two. Willa had wanted to combine the classes which had graduated before and after them to bring the total closer to forty, but she had been shot down. She'd also suggested they could invite their children and grandchildren, but that idea had been nixed, as well.

The three senior ladies had managed to hang some streamers from the wall. Willa had spent the better part of three afternoons on her hands and knees cutting out silhouettes of poodles, dancing figures and a jukebox from black butcher paper, all of which now hung on the walls. Edith's son came with a ladder to hang streamers from the scoreboard and LP records she'd found at a garage sale along the wall as a banner. He turned out to be quite pleasant, much the opposite of his mother.

She'd decorated the tables with black-and-white checkered tablecloths. For the centerpieces, she placed straws and pink and white frilly carnations into old-fashioned soda glasses. It was the best she could do with such limited resources, of the monetary and human nature, and she was proud of her work.

Her favorite, though, was the table she'd just finished. Her cousin in Idaho said they used the boxes with the fancy name plates at her last reunion and it was a huge hit. The idea was that each of the attendees would write a compliment, memory, or words of encouragement on slips of paper for every other attendee and place them in a box labeled with each classmate's name. Then the boxes would go home with each graduate to be enjoyed and cherished later on.

Willa had brought up the idea at the last organizational breakfast, which consisted of six of the classmates meeting at the local diner for an hour, mostly complaining about politics and their Millennial grandchildren. Everyone but Edith thought the idea was fabulous, because everyone but Edith was sentimental about their high school days. Edith had insisted the money to purchase said boxes, the paper and the décor for that table not be taken out of the general fund.

Willa had agreed to foot the bill for it herself. Many of their classmates had lost a spouse or two. Willa's husband of 48 years had added to the list a couple of months ago. Some had lost children—and one should never have to outlive a child. They'd all lost classmates that they had once been close to. Many of these losses had occurred in the last few months. She hoped the boxes would bring a bit of joy to some of the gloom that seemed to surround the aging Nighthawks of 1967.

Barry's treatment was going well, and she'd thought she would attend this milestone with her husband. After his death, she'd needed an outlet, so she had thrown herself into the prep and planning. Aside from Edith, the activity had worked to keep her mind from sorrow and her hands from boredom.

Willa straightened the name plates in front of the boxes. Her cousin had mailed her the mini chalkboards that her class had used for her reunion last month. She wrote each classmate's name in cursive on the boards. She'd spent another few afternoons wrapping each box in fifties paper- poodles for the ladies and records for the guys. She cut four-inch slits in the box tops for the well-wishes and purchased packs of plain white index cards and scattered ink pens along the edge. She even made a couple of extra boxes in case they had a surprise visitor. She tucked those under the table.

After propping each chalkboard in front of a box, satisfied that everything was as ready as it could be, Willa and the other ladies locked up the gym and stepped into the bright blue noonday until the festivities later that evening.

---

"You do realize now that *she* showed up and brought that man with her that the count is off and we may not have enough dessert?" Edith followed Willa into the tiny cafeteria

off the gymnasium. Willa thought about breaking into an all-out sprint, but she was sure Edith's tongue was faster. "What do you propose we do?"

Nulltown was a place that showed up on some maps, but not all. You either found yourself there with a purpose, or you were completely lost. The committee had contacted every living class member via phone to get a head count because there was no supermarket close by, and no commerce in the town to run to for extra supplies or food to match their theme.

"I've already set up a note box for her up front. As for dessert, I guess I'll pass on my slice of five-hundred-calorie cake." She eyed her rival up and down. "Maybe you should do the same, Edith."

Edith left the cafeteria with a huff and her nose in the air. Willa knew it was a cruel thing to say, but she'd had enough. And now she'd have to face Cynthia.

Three months ago, Willa had contacted the classmates with last names of A through D for RSVPs, and, much to Willa's relief, Cynthia Conner-Conrad (or was it Calloway now?) turned down the invitation as she had an out-of-town wedding the weekend before. Her own wedding. Her *fourth* wedding.

And now, it seemed that Cynthia wanted to show off her newest catch. A much younger catch. The woman made Willa's skin crawl.

Cynthia Conner had been Nulltown High's drama queen and boyfriend-stealer, which had been pretty easy given that Cynthia, by far, had had the best-developed body of any of the girls in their class, or the classes ahead of or behind them. She'd flirt with anything that had breath, including the teachers. Poor Mr. Sweltz had succumbed to her ways after English class one afternoon and had been quietly relocated to another district within the week.

Willa slid the specialty cake onto a stainless-steel cart to wheel out to the refreshment table. She backed through the cafeteria's swinging door and into the dimly lit gymnasium where her granddaughter's iPod blasted the decade's hits through a borrowed sound system. Some guests were dancing. Most were sitting. There were a few oxygen tanks in the mix. Cynthia and several others were at the front table, writing away and stuffing the notes into the boxes. Willa tried to control her reaction, but she slid the cake from the cart a little too fast. Her hand slipped off the edge, smearing the purple poodle in the corner.

Cynthia had snagged Edith's beaus twice. She'd tried to do the same with Willa's, but Barry Everly had been a gentleman, even at sixteen years old, and Barry and Willa had married soon after high school.

She and Barry had had a good life. A couple of kids, and now a few grandchildren. She didn't know why something that happened over fifty years ago could bring her so much angst. Cynthia was always the furthest thing from her mind until reunion time crept up every five to ten years or so, when Willa would learn of her current position on the divorce/marriage merry-go-round. One or two "loves of her life" had succumbed to an early demise. You'd think Cynthia'd just give up already.

Willa tried to wipe the poodle from her hand, but the purple icing caked under her thumbnail. She straightened her dress, tucked a strand of hair behind her ear, and summoned the gumption to greet Cynthia and her newest beloved.

"How are you, Cynthia? I'm so glad you decided to come." *Lie.*

"I'm well. I'm well. I'd like to introduce you to... well, where'd he go?" Cynthia looked behind her for her husband, who was still at the table with the boxes. "What are you doing, silly? You don't know any of these people. Come meet Willa." She motioned for him to join her.

When he looked up from the table, Willa recognized him immediately and took a step back. In the span of three seconds, the entirety of the last three months of Barry's illness raced to the front of her mind in excruciating detail.

The diagnosis. Cancer.

The prognosis. Good with treatment.

The rapid decline. Unexplained.

His last heartbeat as she'd rested her head on his chest that evening.

And standing in front of her now was one of Barry's hospice aides. A man twenty years Cynthia's junior. Here. At Nulltown High.

"Isn't he just grand?" She leaned into his shoulder. "We met all the way up in Canton at the University a few months ago. This is James. James, this is Willa."

James reached out his hand. "Nice to meet you. Nice job with the decorations." He turned to Cynthia. "Want some cake and punch, sweetheart?"

"I'd love some." Cynthia patted James on the rear as he walked away.

James clearly didn't recognize Willa, and for that she was glad. James had been the last hospice worker in their home before Barry had passed.

"You okay, love? You look a bit peaked." Cynthia reached out to put a hand on Willa's shoulder.

"Yeah, just a little stuffy in here." *Recover. Recover.* "I am glad you could make it, though. And congratulations on the wedding." She nodded toward the table where James was setting up the couple's refreshments. "It looks like he's quite the catch."

She started toward James. "He is, thank you. Oh, and Willa?"

"Yeah?"

"Sorry to hear about Barry. That's such a shame."

Willa couldn't read the tone. She didn't know whether Cynthia was being sincere or snide. She nodded and smiled at her and headed to straighten the boxes and notecards. When that didn't take as long as she needed it to for the sweaty shakes to subside, she headed for the hallway entrance to catch her breath.

On her way past Edith's table, Willa noticed Edith had taken two pieces of cake.

On her way past the newlyweds' table, Cynthia kissed James on the cheek, then locked eyes with Willa, grinning. The look drilled straight through her heart.

At home in the tranquility of her living room, wearing one of Barry's blue dress shirts, Willa sat cross-legged on the floor with her poodle-covered compliment box. Her cat slinked from behind the couch and loved on the corner of the box, leaving tan and black hairs sticking from the sides.

"Want to help?" She reached out and rubbed his chin.

He purred next to her, and she removed the wrapping paper, tossing it away from the box. Buddy crouched, then pounced, reaching under the paper for some invisible mouse, then walking on top of the crackling mess before curling up in a ball on it. She smiled at him and dumped the note cards onto the floor.

She really had enjoyed seeing her classmates. As she read the cards, most of them were similar. How she'd encouraged them during class. How Barry and she had made such a sweet couple. How sorry they were for her loss. A few told anecdotes that Willa had long forgotten. Some people signed their names to the greetings, others didn't.

She wiped a few tears and reached for the last notecard.

*If I couldn't have him, why should you?*
*Cynthia.*

# STONE STILL

*How far would you go—or how still would you stay—to help an acquaintance? First seen in Ellery Queen Mystery Magazine.*

Sterling Moore arrived at Roberts Park just as the sun's morning rays kissed the tops of the pine trees near the playground. Stray joggers and a solo groundskeeper—all accustomed to the looks of Sterling—all of them dutifully ignored him as they went about their business in the small city park. Beyond the pines, the skyscrapers scratched through the wisps of fog the sun hadn't managed to burn off yet. It would be hot today.

It was hot yesterday. But what did one expect in the middle of June?

How did Moses do this? Day after day in all this gear?

Sterling reached beneath the heavy cloak and retrieved a water bottle, sweaty with condensation. Careful not to let the drops fall on his face, he took in half the bottle in a few giant swigs, then tucked it back in the stiff coat opposite the side of his holstered Glock.

He spotted Moses's bench and made his way toward it, regretting that the sun would be directly in his eyes in a few moments. The pine branches, frail tendrils as they were, would be of no help shading out the rays. He placed the wooden box with the slit in the top near the bench's front foot, just as Moses had done for over a year.

Visible, but not right away.

As Moses had done, so would Sterling. He'd match the man's actions as closely as he could. The bench. The box. The costume—uniform as Moses had called it in his letter.

And the pose.

Sterling adjusted his stiff coverings and draped his arm over the back of the bench. The other, and this is where his pose differed from Moses, rested on the water bottle inside the heavy coverings. He crossed his legs, allowing the bronzed leggings and one-size-too small stiff shoes to poke from under the coat.

He fixed his gaze on the swing set.

No. That would be no good. The swing would be in motion soon as squealing children filled the playground.

The pines? The faint breeze, scant in strength and frequency, caused the branches to bend just a little. Still too much motion for Sterling's liking.

Sometimes, when one stared at inanimate objects with intricate patterns, such as the bark of the massive oak towering fifty yards from the bench, those patterns jump out in a twisting three-dimensional illusion, causing one to blink far too often if one were to be a statue. The bark of the oak was already doing that to him, and he'd only considered the trunk of the tree for a few seconds.

He blinked hard, resetting his field of vision to baseline.

The twisty slide would work. The tip of the safety rail.

He fixed his gaze on the top of the slide so his eyes would remain still. He hoped the Tudor hat with long bronzed feather didn't melt off his head, revealing his high-and-tight officer cut. He'd not bothered to apply the bronzing solution to the portion of his head where the hat covered. Moses's supply was running low, and that stage makeup, after much research by his department, was exuberantly expensive.

Officer Sterling Moore was as close to a living statue as a first-time, untrained street artist could be. He spent the past several nights awake, restless. Playing over and over in his mind what he may have missed during his patrols of Roberts Park in the days prior. Unwilling to shake the disappearance of Moses. A man who'd never spoken a word to Sterling in all the days on patrol.

But Sterling felt he knew the old man, nonetheless.

Maybe it was the startle Moses had given Sterling almost a year ago. The first time the Shakespearean statue had shown itself in the park. Sterling thought the parks department had installed a new addition. A little culture. A little history.

But there'd been no plaque for the bronze man.

No ribbon-cutting ceremony as there had been when the new Founding Fathers Fountain went in over by the picnic shelters.

Only a tiny, wooden box by stone-still shoes. With a slit in the top.

Then it dawned on Sterling.

Shakespeare—Moses—was a street performer. So still. So perfectly posed in contemplation. No way this poor bloke made any tips—not nearly the tips the other creatives that flocked to Roberts Park took home after a sunny day of work. Not like the break-dancers spinning on their heads, jumping, and flipping. Jugglers. Magicians.

The folky guitarists with smoky voices, lyrics spilling out that the gals and guys no doubt poured heart and soul in. Some were okay. Some were surprisingly good. Most were homeless or nearly there.

Sterling gave himself and the costume one more adjustment before going into sniper mode. Before his tour with the police force, Sterling had plenty of practice remaining stone still for long periods of time, usually on his belly, though, peering through the scope of his rifle. Definitely not covered in stage makeup, balancing a feathered cap on his head, and eyeing a twisty slide.

The training returned. Breathe in, breathe out. Ignore the sweat beads tickling the forehead and temples. Allow no motion.

Hold the bladder. Ignore the fatigue.

Ignore the flies.

Ignore the heat or the cold or the wind or whatever the weather dealt during his assignments.

Fixate on the target. A doorway. A window.

A slide.

He let his mind wander as the foot traffic increased. Children. Parents. Joggers. Lovers hand in hand enjoying the performances. Those who knew about the nature of the park brought pockets full of dollar bills. Sterling earned a dollar every half hour or so. Lots of selfies, ladies cuddling up into his side. Shakespeare himself draped an arm around a lucky few.

He knew from his patrol the other performers with open guitar cases and upside-down top hats earned far more after their gigs played through. Moses, well. Sterling and the other guys couldn't understand how the man afforded his loft a few blocks away. Let alone all the artifacts inside. At least not yet.

Sterling was the one who insisted the department at least spend some time looking into the disappearance of this stone silent man. Street performers came and went, but were usually found pretty quickly. A park across the city—new grounds with new audiences and other wallets to explore. Some, the younger ones, packed it up and went home to mommy's basement. Others weren't so lucky.

After the deaths of several street folks over the sweltering summer, Sterling wanted to investigate the missing statue.

And after the note discovered in Moses's loft. Well... when they found the note, the captain allotted just a few more resources. Some of those very resources were smeared all over Sterling's face, hands, and legs. Draped over his shoulders and laced to his feet.

The sun beat from overhead now. Nearly noon. A couple of mothers drug screaming children away from the slide and swings. Time for lunch. Time to go.

One kid wailed and wailed at the massive oak tree, pointing. Screaming. Sterling couldn't help but look, the law enforcement training overtaking the need to keep his eyes fixed. Sterling didn't see anything but that three-dimensional illusion in the bark, and the mother scooped up the boy and walked to her car. The kid probably wanted to take a squirrel home.

Or was terrified of squirrels.

He blinked hard, wetting his eyes and allowing the orbs to take in the fullness of the park. Give the muscles a break.

Trash here and there around the playground. A beach ball rolling toward the line of pines. An abandoned baseball bat and toy truck near the base of the oak.

After a few more glances and gentle nods to his co-workers, Sterling straightened a kink out of his back, took a swig of the water, and resumed the position. Other performers were resetting as well. Changing music tracks, readjusting props, and replacing guitar strings as the crowd lightened ever so slightly for the moment.

He'd been called in a few times to settle territory disputes, especially when word got out that talent scouts or casting directors would be in the area. Tip jars, punches, and foul language spilled along the park's concrete pathways on those days.

Sitting here, though, Sterling had to wonder what Moses had done. Had seen. Had possessed. The note Moses left was vague. A plea for help in plain English. He'd been scared for his life, he said. And it'd mentioned "Officer Moore with that Nag of a Wife." With the caps in all the right places.

Sterling's superior officer was shocked. "Well, you know. I spend so much time patrolling. I'd sit and chat with the old guy. Tell him stories..." Sterling had tried to offer an explanation, but what could he say?

He'd sat on this very bench close to Shakespeare—not quite tucked into Moses's armpit as the selfie-takers had been—but close enough for a one-sided conversation.

The bench visits started as a joke. "How, ya doin' today, ol' Bard?" or "How goes Juliette these days?"

Moses remained still. Shakespeare never spoke. Never blinked.

Then Sterling took to memorizing famous quotes. "All that glitters is not gold." The quotes earned Sterling a nearly imperceptible nod of the head. Then Moses would return to statuesque mode.

Over the weeks, the jabs and quotes turned into one-sided chats on the bench. Sterling opened up and Moses/Shakespeare listened. No judgment. No eye rolls or head tilts. Someone to unload on and, Sterling was certain, someone that would keep his secrets.

The unpleasable wife. The overbearing mother-in-law. The entitled teenagers.

Moses listened to it all. And Sterling started sliding fives and tens into Moses's tip box for the therapy sessions.

Two curious preschoolers interrupted Sterling's thoughts. The pair, a boy and a girl, slid onto the bench. Then a little closer. Then a little closer, until the tiny boy ventured a climb onto the statue, facing the playground, swinging his legs so his tennis shoes pounded against Shakespeare's shins. These two, smelling of French fries and chicken nuggets and much too young for Elizabethan literature, likely thought him to be a rusted Ronald McDonald clown.

The little girl, sweat pasting her blonde locks to her cheeks, went to her knees on the bench and inspected Sterling's face. He tried hard not to smile. No blinking. He held his breath and the boy settled against his chest—dangerously close to his little hip finding the grip of his Glock. He'd have to do something to startle them away before the innocent kids tried to unrobe him.

The little girl poked his cheek. She had to feel the midday-stubble growing through the bronze makeup. "Are you real?"

From his periphery, he saw the mother running toward them. "Oh, no. Get off that! Get off him! OMG, I'm so sorry..."

Sterling couldn't help himself. As the mom approached, he took his eyes off the top of the slide, for a split second, widened them toward the girl, and in his deepest, growly voice, said "Boo."

The kids screamed and scurried toward the mom. Sterling flinched a bit as the boy's elbow flew into his ribs during the dismount. He recovered his straight-face and started at the slide. Mom fished into her pocket and dropped clunking coins into the box at his feet, still gushing apologies and threats of no ice cream for the tots if they didn't listen.

When they were out of sight, a small grin escaped one side of his cheek. He felt the thick paste crack a little. He'd not make it to dusk with much of anything intact.

How did Moses do it?

Therapy sessions. Selfies. Endless days of curious, climbing kids.

Under hot suns and bitter cold clouds. Under layers and layers of stage makeup and costuming.

His partner thought him crazy. Williams worked his way through the park now nonetheless, walking the usual patrol routes, chatting up the dancers and guitarists as he went. Ignoring—as Williams usually did—Shakespeare on the bench. They'd worked out a signal. If Williams spotted anything unusual on his rounds while Sterling sat undercover, he'd leave a tip in the box, Sterling's cue to be alert.

A tip, or a foot chase, whichever happened first. Though with the heavy garb and bad shoes, Sterling doubted he'd be much of a help to Williams if a call came in, a fight broke out, or if they found any kind of suspect in the Moses disappearance.

If Sterling spotted something—well, more likely he'd *hear* something since his eyes remained on the slide's top—he'd drop the water bottle from inside his cloak under the bench. Two other officers, Barry and Michelle, in day clothes and leaving tips here and there for the performers, were also on the lookout for Sterling to drop the bottle.

He envied their freedom. Their ability to walk about and stretch and take a restroom break. To guzzle the cart vendors' sweaty bottles of water and lick mango sorbet from plastic spoons. But this was Sterling's hand-picked case. And he insisted the best way to scope the park wasn't to show photos of Moses in Shakespeare's garb to all of the performers. They'd not rat for fear of retaliation. Theirs was a tight-knit group, even if they didn't like each other.

No. Sterling thought it best to become Moses. Walk in his shoes. Sit on his bench. Stare. Stone still.

And think.

What did he see that day?

The 911 call had come three days prior. Four days prior, Sterling noticed Moses hadn't shown up to his post. No tip box. No bronze residue. No witty Bard for a much-needed one-sided banter.

The call was anonymous. The caller said he'd been chased by a man with a gun. Come quick. Please help. Dispatch had sent out a patrol car to the address. An industrial studio loft a few blocks from the park. No one was there when the police arrived.

Cases of makeup, props, costumes, and robes littered the walkways and countertops. Larger props hung from the ceiling by ropes and chains: sleighs, swords, backdrops, artificial greenery in all species of flora. By any therapists' standards, Moses was a hoarder of all things theater.

The note rested on the table next to a box of bronzing powder and a dish of half-eaten scrambled eggs and toast.

"They think I saw something. Please help." Addressed to the officer with the nag of a wife.

The joke down at the precinct was that if Moses's note hadn't mentioned Sterling by name, it could've indicated any of the married police officers. Except Barry. His wife was still perfectly perfect after three fresh months of marriage.

Newlywedded bliss. It would pass.

Sterling almost grinned again, but stifled it, lest half of his face fall off in plaster-like chunks to his lap. He swore the sweat was running, but there wasn't anything he could do about it. Maybe it wasn't running. Maybe it was pooling in pockets under the stage makeup and was about to erupt in mini geysers from his face and neck.

Hours on this bench. In this position. It rivaled anything he'd ever done as a sniper on his stomach perches.

Over the last few hours, a few more selfies, another curious toddler—this time he refrained from spooking the kid—and one chatty old woman. Not chatting at him, per se, but likely a light case of Alzheimer's as a middle-aged couple came running to her, gently cupping her elbows, and led her off to the nearby apartment complex.

Had Moses known of that woman? Did he keep an eye on her in her demented wanderings?

Sterling liked to think so.

Someone slid to the end of the bench. A couple of feet from him. Sterling kept his eyes on the slide, grateful the sun was behind him now instead of bouncing laser beams off the metal fixtures of the playground. The pines were still. No sweat-whisking breeze, unfortunately, and he hoped this visitor couldn't smell his sweat.

Peripheral vision of the oak tree did that crazy three-dimensional thing again, and Sterling thought he noticed movement around the trunk. But all the children had gone home for family time, or more likely screen time, and he had to struggle not to blink away the phenomenon.

His guest was a male. Bald. Overalls. Staring right at his face. Scooting closer and closer.

Waving a hand in front of his eyes.

Sterling didn't blink.

Kicking gently at his shoes.

Sterling didn't move.

"I guess you're gonna want a tip, huh, Moses?"

Sterling remained still.

"Guess you don't understand simple orders, huh, Moses?" He scooted even closer. Nearly in Sterling's armpit. The man smelled of weed and alcohol. Sterling's grip around the water bottle tightened, and he hoped it wouldn't crackle the plastic.

Then pressure. Near the ribs. Pressing through the cloak and into his skin. A blade. Sharp enough to penetrate all those bronzed layers.

Why hadn't he worn his Kevlar?

Heat, dummy. That's why. It was too hot.

He removed his gaze from the slide. Slowly. A little nearer.

To the oak tree. Movement there, too, but Sterling couldn't process it. The blade was at the perfect lung-puncturing angle, and that's where his eyes dropped to, watering from all the staring and lack of blinking.

"How about we go for a walk, Shakespeare?" The hatred dripped off his words, the knife pressed in deeper. Through the undershirt.

A whoosh drew his attention up as he dropped the water bottle from under the cloak. The oak tree. The three-dimensional aura Sterling had wrestled out of his sight so many times that day stood behind the bench, wielding the abandoned baseball bat, bringing the wood cracking down on the knife guy's head.

The knife remained tangled in the bronzed cloak.

Williams was running.

The plain-clothes officers were running. Yelling. Barry in the lead. Michelle close behind.

Williams drew his weapon, unsure of where to aim. The fallen male or the talking tree trunk with arms and legs.

Hoarse and parched, Sterling stood, although wobbling and nearly tripping over the unconscious man. The knife fell from the cloak and clanked to the pavement. The Tudor slid off the back of his head and landed on the guy's gut. "Stop. Stop. Weapons down." He kicked the knife away with his bronzy shoe.

The tree trunk dropped the ball bat as Williams moved to cover this strange sight.

Sterling rubbed his eyes, putting more bronze in than getting grit out. "Moses?"

"He's the bad guy, Boss." Moses nodded to the man on the ground, sweat streaking through his oak-bark face paint. "I saw him one night I did. I saw him rob those ladies. Hurt them bad by the pine trees, and I was gonna call you. He knew. He'd seen you on the bench with me that day."

Moses pulled off the shroud of camouflaged bark covering his shoulder. He was in a gray T-shirt underneath. Short sleeved. A wound, straight and angry, a few days old, snaked up from his elbow to under the sleeve cuff. "He got me good." He hung his head. "I got scared and abandoned my station. That was my bad, Boss."

Sterling's head spun. From the sitting. From the scene before him. Gawkers lined up in semi-circles to do the tech thing. Phones out. Recording. Snapping. Chatting. Barry cuffed the unconscious man.

Michelle and Williams attempted to keep the crowd back.

Sterling sat down on the bench again, but in his own usual spot, not Shakespeare's. He motioned for Moses to join him. In seamless movement, Moses sat, legs crossed and arm draped over the back of the bench. The pose of The Bard.

"You'll have to tell us this down at the station. Give a statement."

Moses nodded.

"You'll need medical attention for that cut. Antibiotics."

Moses nodded.

They sat there for a minute, Sterling catching his breath and his wits. Moses staring off into the distance. "How'd you know I'd come looking for you?"

Moses grinned and made full eye contact with Sterling. Kind brown eyes behind stage paint. Crazy dark curls. Sterling wondered how long it took him to tuck them all away for the Shakespeare costume.

"That wife of yours. I knew you'd need to unload soon."

Sterling guffawed and sat back on the bench, shaking his head.

Williams had brought his squad around. A few fellow officers came along with the paramedics. They bagged the bat. The knife. Moses's camouflaged shroud.

The paramedics brought fresh water for the two on the bench.

"Hey, Boss?"

"Yeah, Moses." Sterling had already downed the water.

"Can I have my hat back?"

Sterling scooped the feathered Tudor from under the bench and handed it to Moses. The veteran street performer adjusted it on his head, draped his arm in its rightful position, and stared up toward the dusky sky. Still as a statue.

Officer Sterling Moore, untrained street artist, full-time officer, watched four men lift the perp into the back of an ambulance. The criminal didn't call out. Didn't flinch. Save for a small trickle of blood staining the white sheet by his head, the guy was stone still.

# ABOUT THE AUTHOR

Beth enjoys chucking words into sentences then standing back to see what magic—or mayhem—falls out, crafting tales in mystery, sci-fi, fantasy, and general "slice of life" fiction. She couldn't accomplish this without the help of her tutu-clad Little Miss Muse and Trudi the Concrete Office Goose, who's partial to superhero capes.

Her stories have appeared in multiple publications, including Pulphouse Fiction Magazine and Ellery Queen Mystery Magazine, and in multiple fiction anthologies. She's received several Honorable Mentions from Writers of the Future. Her lighthearted blog peeks into the writing life as she pokes fun at herself and her circus of a life.

Follow the antics of Little Miss Muse and Trudi, read Beth's blog (she might have burned down her kitchen last week), and discover the stories at bapaul.com.

# Stay In Touch!

BAPAUL.COM

Take a glimpse into B.A. Paul's writing journey, including the ups and downs of managing family, "real jobs," ducks in wobbling rows, and chasing down her Little Miss Muse. New blog posts go up Mondays, with the first Monday of the Month reserved for a free fiction short story available on the blog for a limited time.

Newsletter Signup!

Get the latest release information, author updates, and exclusive content by signing up with your email. Check out bapaul.com.